GOOD D:2:G

Raised in a Barn

by
Cam Higgins

illustrated by
Ariel Landy

LITTLE SIMON

New York London Toronto Sydney New Delhi

This book is a work of fiction. Any references to historical events, real people, or real places are used fictitiously. Other names, characters, places, and events are products of the author's imagination, and any resemblance to actual events or places or persons, living or dead, is entirely coincidental.

LITTLE SIMON

An imprint of Simon & Schuster Children's Publishing Division
1230 Avenue of the Americas, New York, New York 10020
First Little Simon paperback edition December 2020
Copyright © 2020 by Simon & Schuster, Inc.
Also available in a Little Simon hardcover edition.
All rights reserved, including the right of reproduction in whole or in part in any form. LITTLE SIMON is a registered trademark of Simon & Schuster, Inc., and associated colophon is a trademark of Simon & Schuster, Inc.
For information about special discounts for bulk purchases, please contact Simon & Schuster Special Sales at 1-866-506-1949
or business@simonandschuster.com.
The Simon & Schuster Speakers Bureau can bring authors to your live event. For more information or to book an event contact the
Simon & Schuster Speakers Bureau at 1-866-248-3049 or visit our website at www.simonspeakers.com.
Designed by Leslie Mechanic
Manufactured in the United States of America 1120 MTN
10 9 8 7 6 5 4 3 2 1
Library of Congress Cataloging-in-Publication Data
Names: Higgins, Cam, author. | Landy, Ariel, illustrator.
Title: Raised in a barn / by Cam Higgins; illustrated by Ariel Landy.
Description: New York: Little Simon, 2020 | Series: Good dog; 2 | Audience: Ages 5–9. | Audience: Grades K–1. | Summary: Farm puppy Bo introduces a young foal to life on the farm.
Identifiers: LCCN 2020045382 | ISBN 9781534479036 (paperback) | ISBN 9781534479043 (hardcover) | ISBN 9781534479050 (eBook)
Subjects: CYAC: Dogs—Fiction. | Horses—Fiction. | Animals—Infancy—Fiction. | Farm life—Fiction.
Classification: LCC PZ7.1.H54497 Rai 2020 | DDC [Fic]—dc23
LC record available at https://lccn.loc.gov/2020045382

CONTENTS

Comet

The sky was a clear blue. Puffs of fluffy white clouds drifted above the Davis farm. The sunshine made the fur on my back feel nice and warm. Even the dirt smelled yummy, like leaves, flowers, and mud. I dug my paws deeper into the ground.

It was the perfect day for a race!

Comet came bounding out of the barn. Her horse legs still seemed a little bit too long for her horse body as she trotted over to me.

Comet is the new horse. She is Star and Grey's foal, and she thinks she's fast.

But I'm Bo Davis! Everyone knows I am the fastest animal around.

I can run faster than a chicken. I can run faster than a sheep. I can even run faster than my human brother and sister, Wyatt and Imani.

Plus, I can almost outrun the family truck, if it weren't for the fence I'm not supposed to cross.

That's why Comet and I needed to race: to prove once and for all who's the fastest on the Davis farm.

I greeted the young horse with a nod. "Morning, Comet."

"Hiya, Bo," she neighed cheerfully. "What a nice, sunny day!"

"It sure is," I said. "Are you ready to run?"

"You bet I am! And I'm going to win, too!" Comet said.

I woofed with a big puppy dog grin.

"Oh, Comet, I'm sorry, but I don't think so. I've been running since before you were born!"

Some of the sheep grazing in the field nearby lifted their heads and watched us. Zonks the pig glanced up from his trough and shuffled over.

"Wait, are you two racing?" he squealed. Then he hollered, "Hey, everyone! Bo and Comet are going to see who's faster—horses or dogs!"

Well, that was all the farm needed to hear. Soon all sorts of animals gathered around us.

Suddenly chickens, cows, sheep, and ducks were bickering about who they thought would win the race.

I could feel my heart beat a little bit quicker. We had an audience!

I tried to ignore everyone else and asked, "Where should we race to, Comet?"

She looked around the pasture, then lifted her nose toward the far end of the field.

"How about we race to that bale of hay down there?" Comet suggested.

"Okay," I agreed. "Where should we start?"

Before Comet could answer, Rufus the rooster strutted over.

Rufus was the head rooster, and where he went, animals paid attention.

He scratched a line in the dirt and clucked, "You will start here. Now take your marks, get set, and wait for my signal."

Horsing Around

As Comet and I stood next to each other, the rest of the farm animals lined the racecourse.

Comet arched her neck, then stuck it out straight and long. She was ready to dash.

I crouched low too and prepared to run as fast as I could.

Rufus counted down. "Okay. Three, two, one, cock-a-doodle-doo!"

I bounded out first, but I could feel Comet's hooves thumping the ground close behind me.

My legs stretched out as far as they could reach, and I moved through the air. I was almost floating, but I felt the grass tickle the pads of my paws.

The entire farm zipped by me. Or I zipped past it. Running like this makes dogs feel freer and happier than ever.

But Comet was still right behind me. She was fast for a foal!

I knew horses were good runners, but I didn't think she would be *this* speedy.

Then Comet wasn't behind me anymore. She was right next to me!

"Hi, Bo," she neighed.

Comet wasn't out of breath at all! My tongue was hanging out, and I was panting for air, but Comet looked like she could run forever.

She smiled and said, "Bo, can you believe all the animals have come out to see us? And look at those pretty flowers!"

I didn't answer. I just watched that bale of hay coming closer and closer. But a loud squawk startled me.

A baby chick had wandered into the middle of our race! I bolted into the air and avoided a bad crash.

Those free-range chickens always get in the way!

Now Comet edged in front of me. Her legs pumped so fast that I knew the race was over. All I could do was watch her mane stream out behind her.

Then she slammed on the brakes and stopped!

This was my chance. I ran and ran until I reached that hay bale first.

I hopped up on top of it, lifted my nose in the air, and howled with joy. "I'm so fast, no little foal could ever beat me."

Nanny Sheep stepped out from behind the bale. She wore a frown and baaed in disappointment.

"Bo," she said, "you are behaving foolishly. A good sports-pup never teases other animals, whether you win or lose. I know Comet seems like a big horse, but she's still very young, and she has a lot to learn. Now go apologize."

I wasn't sure what Nanny Sheep meant by Comet still having a lot to learn. But I hung my head in shame. I hadn't meant to tease Comet or make her feel bad. Running just made me feel so good, and winning made me feel even better.

I found Comet sniffing the tall grass.

"Hey, Comet," I said. "I'm sorry for acting kind of mean when I won the race."

"It's okay, Bo," Comet said brightly. "Look what I found!"

With a toss of her head, Comet nodded toward a butterfly resting on a flower. Its wings slowly fluttered open and closed.

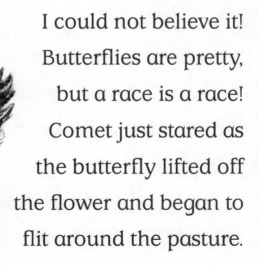

"Comet," I barked, "it's just a butterfly! You stopped running the race for that?"

I could not believe it! Butterflies are pretty, but a race is a race! Comet just stared as the butterfly lifted off the flower and began to flit around the pasture.

The young horse hopped after it, prancing around with her mouth wide open.

"Wow!" Comet said . . . until her mouth snapped shut and the butterfly was gone.

"Did you just eat the butterfly?!" I yelped. "We don't eat butterflies!"

Comet looked up at me guiltily, then opened her mouth.

The butterfly flew out quickly, shaking his head and grumbling under his breath about foals who need to learn their manners.

Gosh, maybe this is what Nanny Sheep meant when she said Comet still had a lot to learn.

Coach
Bo

I took a long nap after the race.
When I woke up later, I had lunch
with Wyatt and Imani. Then my best
puppy friend, Scrapper, came over
for a visit.

We went out to the woods to search
for his monster. Now, I've never seen
a monster there, but Scrapper has.

And he's been trying to find it again
ever since.

As we walked, I told Scrapper all
about the race.

"A chick ducked into my path. Hey,
the chick *ducked*. Get it?" I barked
with a giggle.

Scrapper woofed. "That's funny,
Bo!"

I kept on with my story. "Well, that chick slowed me down, and Comet pulled ahead. But then—"

Scrapper interrupted me. "Look, Bo! Did you see that over there?"

"See what?" I replied.

"That! Over there," he whispered. "Maybe it's a—"

We looked at each other and shouted together, "SQUIRREL!"

Sure enough, a squirrel was by the trees looking for nuts. We took off, and as soon as that squirrel saw us coming, he took off too. Right up a tree trunk and onto a branch that hung high over our heads.

Scrapper and I looked up and barked our heads off.

When we were sure the squirrel was gone, we continued on our way.

I sniffed the ground and kept a close eye out for more squirrels—and for Scrapper's monster, too.

"So, what happened, Bo?" Scrapper asked.

"Huh?" I said. "Oh, you mean with Comet? She stopped in the middle of the race to chase a—get this—a butterfly!"

"What? A butterfly?" Scrapper said wonderingly.

"Can you believe it?" I asked. "That poor foal doesn't know the first thing about being a horse!"

"Oooh, look over there!" Scrapper pushed his nose forward, and I could see a long shadow slipping between the trees.

"The monster!" we both said at the same time. We started to run toward it.

"Hey there, Mr. Monster, wait up!" Scrapper barked.

But it wasn't a monster. It was Imani and Wyatt.

"Hey, boy," Wyatt said, bending to scratch me behind my ears. He knows exactly where my favorite spot is.

"Are you and Scrapper hunting squirrels?" Imani leaned down to pat Scrapper.

I woofed to ask if they wanted to join, but I don't think they did. Humans just don't understand how important it is to chase squirrels.

"We have to go, but look, Bo," said Imani. She picked up a stick off the ground and tossed it through the air. "Fetch!"

Scrapper and I reached the stick at the same time and played a little game of tug-of-war until we got tired.

"You know," Scrapper said, "maybe Comet could be a great horse if she had the right teacher."

That gave me a bright idea!

"I think you're right, Scrapper," I told him. "Comet could use someone who knows about life on the farm."

"Yeah," Scrapper agreed. "Someone who is kind and honest and who will tell her when she makes a mistake."

I felt a big doggy grin spreading over my face. "I know the perfect teacher for Comet! Someone who knows all about the farm and who is always nice to her."

"Who's that?" asked Scrapper.

"Me!" I howled.

First Things
First

I woke up early the next morning and went straight to the barn.

The first thing Comet needed to learn was that farm animals never sleep in.

"Wakey, wakey, Comet!" I called. "Time to rise and shine!"

Comet peeked her sleepy head out.

Then she yawned. "Bo? Are you in my dream?"

"You're not dreaming," I cheered. "It's morning, and you have horse lessons!"

"Horse lessons?" Comet asked.

I puffed out my chest. "Yep, you lucky foal! I'm going to teach you everything you need to know about being a horse. Now let's go eat."

Comet opened both eyes wide to stare at me. "What are you talking about?"

"I am talking about eating," I explained. "Humans eat in the house, and horses eat in the barn."

I walked over to the haystack and pulled a small clump of hay loose. "Here's some breakfast for you. Horses eat hay."

"I know how to eat, Bo," Comet huffed. "But thanks for the hay. I am pretty hungry."

She dipped her head and began to munch.

When she finished, I said, "Next, we take a morning walk. Because, um . . . well, because Mother Nature calls."

I headed out to the meadow, but
Comet wasn't following me.

"Aren't you coming?" I asked.

"Um, Bo," she called from inside the
barn, "is it safe to come out? Did you
already, um, call on Mother Nature?"

I trotted back to the barn. I could

feel my cheeks getting warm under my fur. Comet sure wasn't making this any easier. "Oh, uh, yeah, I already went. But do you . . . ?"

Comet giggled. "I'm okay, but maybe we can just skip past this part of the lesson?"

Phew. What a relief.

"Yes, we can definitely skip past this and go on to the next lesson!" I said.

"What is it?" Comet asked.

"Uh, well . . . huh." I had no idea what should come next. "What do horses do all day?" I asked Comet.

"We like to take walks—*real* walks— to stretch our legs in the morning," Comet answered.

"A walk! Perfect!" I exclaimed. "Let's do that!"

5

Hold
Your Horses

Comet and I headed into the delicious spring sunshine. As we walked, I pointed out some animals that were not from the farm.

"Look, Comet, see those evil guys with the big fluffy tails?" I asked.

A pair of chattering gray squirrels sat in the meadow.

They were probably planning something bad. I just knew it. You can't trust a squirrel.

"Those are squirrels," I explained. "We chase them, but they are really fast."

Oh, I could feel my legs itching to run after them.

"Okay. But why do you chase the squirrels?" Comet asked. "Have they done anything wrong?"

"Not yet," I replied quickly. "That's why we chase them. So they don't have a chance to do anything wrong."

Comet looked at me, then nodded slowly. "In that case, let's go!"

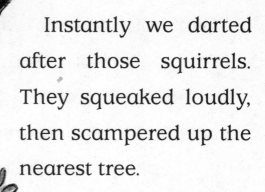

Instantly we darted after those squirrels. They squeaked loudly, then scampered up the nearest tree.

"That was some good squirrel chasing," I told Comet.

Suddenly a soft tweet came from above us. I looked up, and it was Blue the blue jay.

"Hi, Blue!" I called.

Blue waved his wing down to us.

"That's Blue," I explained to Comet. "He's a bird. Birds build nests in the

tree branches, and they mostly eat worms."

Comet neighed softly.

"Make sure you don't mix up birds and bats. Bats only come out at night," I told her. "They live in a bat house on top of the barn, and they're very helpful. They eat farm pests like moths and mosquitoes."

"I didn't know that," Comet said. "Do they eat flies? Those are the worst pests."

"Gosh, I don't know," I admitted.

Then I looked over at Comet and noticed her flicking her tail back and forth. She even swatted at her own back with it.

"What are you doing with your tail there?" I asked.

"I'm keeping the flies off me," she explained. "They're always bugging me and making my coat itch."

"Oh, I know how to keep the flies away," I said. "Look!"

I began rolling all over the ground.

"See how I roll back and forth in the dust?" I asked. "It feels good and scares the flies!"

"Let me try!" Comet said.

She lowered herself to the ground and began to roll. Then she started to giggle.

Pretty soon we were both laughing and rolling, kicking up small clouds of dust. Or maybe not so small.

Comet's parents, Star and Grey, trotted over and shouted, "Hold your horses, Comet!"

Uh-oh. I took one look at their long faces and knew that Comet's parents were not happy. Not one little bit.

6

Barn Hair, Don't Care

"What in the world are you doing?" Star whinnied.

"Bo is giving me horse lessons," Comet explained. "Rolling around on the ground is how horses keep flies away."

Star and Grey let out great big sighs.

"Comet," Grey said in a gentle voice, "horses don't roll on the ground to get rid of flies. We were worried you might be hurt!"

Then Star added, "It is very nice of Bo to help. But maybe he isn't the best animal to teach you about being a horse."

Hmm, I thought. "Star has a point. As a dog, maybe I don't really know how to be a horse."

Comet stood up, and her parents gasped. Comet's mane was a mess. It was tangled and dirty.

"Oh dear," said Star. "You were supposed to keep clean for the foal parade!"

"Parade?" I asked. "What parade?"

"There is a special parade for young foals at a local fair," said Grey. "Wyatt and Imani have worked so hard to groom Comet, getting her ready. But now they'll have to start all over again. Luckily, the parade isn't until tomorrow."

"So we have time," I woofed.

"Yes," said Star. "How about everyone comes into the barn, and we'll see what we can do about Comet's mane? Maybe Nanny Sheep knows a trick we can use."

As we all headed back to the barn, I saw two slim shadows slip inside first.

King and Diva. Those two barn cats always turn up when we least expect them.

"Oooh, Comet," Diva hissed from rafters at the top of the barn. "We love what you did for your hair."

"Yessss," King joined in. "That hairstyle is for the birds. Because it looks like a nest!"

Both cats cackled loudly and just about fell out of the rafters.

Comet hung her head and neighed softly. She seemed so sad, and those cats were not helping her feel any better.

"Hey!" I woofed at the cats. "You two had better cut it out!"

"Oh no, it's Bo, and he's barking mad," Diva meowed. "Can't Comet speak for herself? No, of course she can't! She's just a little baby horse!"

Before I knew what I was doing,
I jumped up the steps to the hayloft
and scared those cats. King and Diva
darted out the window with a hiss.

Then I heard a new sound. Comet
was crying.

I hopped down the steps and went to her side.

"Please don't let barn cats rain on your parade. They're just jealous," I told her. "You know, there's a saying all farm animals should learn: barn hair, don't care."

Comet sniffled. "What does that mean?"

"It means if you're working hard, then your hair will show it. But if your hair looks super neat, like those silly cats, well, it means you're hardly working at all."

"I like the sound of that," said Comet with a small whinny.

"Besides," I continued, "real farm animals don't care about how you look. They care about how you act."

Now there was a new neighing behind me. Star and Grey were in the doorway.

"You know, Bo, you are absolutely right. Maybe you do know something about horse life," Grey said.

"Now let's see what we can do about that mane," said Star. She trotted over to us and nuzzled Comet lovingly.

7

Horse Show-and-Tell

The next day I woke up as soon as I heard Wyatt and Imani getting dressed. I knew they'd be working with Comet, and I wanted to go too.

I waited while they brushed their teeth and ate breakfast. When they finished, Imani scraped some eggs and bacon into my bowl. Yum!

As soon as the front door opened, I headed straight for the barn. Imani and Wyatt followed behind me.

The foal parade at the local fair was that afternoon. So I knew this morning would be all about getting Comet ready. There would be lots of grooming. I was excited for Comet and wanted to make sure no cats or squirrels bothered her.

Inside the barn, Wyatt pulled down a bridle. It was made of smooth brown leather and looked a lot like a leash.

When the kids showed me a leash, it meant we were going for a walk off the farm, which is one of my most favorite things!

I wanted to jump and howl with happiness, but I stopped myself. Young foals get nervous pretty easily, and I didn't want to bother Comet.

Wyatt gently stroked her nose and reminded her that the bridle would help Imani lead Comet in the parade. Comet whinnied softly and lowered her head.

Wyatt placed the bridle on her while Imani patted Comet's neck and whispered, "Good horse."

I felt my heart swell because Wyatt and Imani knew exactly how to treat Comet, gently and carefully. They probably knew how to care for every animal—whether it's a dog like me, a foal like Comet, or even squirrels.

That's why my humans are the best humans ever.

Next, Imani took a brush down from the shelf and told Comet that it was a soft dandy brush. She held it out so Comet could sniff the bristles. She even held it out for me to give it a sniff too.

I could smell Star's and Grey's and even Comet's scents. Their horsey smell was comforting. I gave a little woof, and Imani giggled.

Then she began to brush Comet from head to tail. She swept it in small, careful circles very slowly so she wouldn't startle Comet.

As I watched Imani brushing, I
imagined the brush sweeping over
my fur, and my back started to feel
just a tiny bit itchy. Maybe tonight the
kids would give me a back scratch.

"There," Imani said when she was done. "You look beautiful, Comet!"

And she really did. Her coat was so glossy, and her mane and tail were smooth and shiny.

"Okay, Comet, are you ready to practice our walk?" Imani asked.

Comet nodded and then followed Imani out of the barn.

Darn
Squirrels

Wyatt walked to a fenced-in area and opened the gate.

The ground was covered in soft sand. I set one paw in it, not sure what it would feel like. The sand shifted under my pads and was almost as cool as mud.

Comet and Imani followed us.

Once they were inside, Wyatt closed the gate behind them. I looked up at Wyatt and tilted my head to the side.

"This is called the school," Wyatt explained. "We bring the horses here to practice riding. The fence keeps them safe, mostly by keeping other animals out. Horses can get nervous, especially

young ones like Comet. So we practice her parade walk in here first."

I wagged my tail. I loved it when Wyatt taught me new things.

We watched Imani lead Comet around the school. She guided the horse gently by the bridle.

After a few laps, Imani gave Comet
a carrot, which the foal gobbled up.

Yum. I was hungry too! I looked at
Wyatt and whimpered.

Wyatt laughed. "Sorry, Bo. Those
treats are for Comet."

I hung my head, but Wyatt quickly
cheered me up.

"Dogs don't eat horse treats, silly. They need dog treats . . . like this one." Then he tossed me a cookie bone!

OH BOY! Helping Comet was delicious.

When practice was done, Imani led Comet out of the school and into the field. They walked back and forth around a water barrel and wove between a line of hay bales.

Comet was doing a great job. That is, until a squirrel showed up!

It bounded through the field just in front of Comet. I felt my legs get ready to spring after it, but Comet beat me to it.

As she pulled away to chase the squirrel, Imani held on to Comet's bridle with both hands and murmured calmly to her. Comet stopped pulling and obediently followed Imani back to the barn.

After Comet was back in her stall, Wyatt patted her nose and told her she did well.

But when we left to help Mom and Dad get the horse trailer, I heard Wyatt whisper to Imani, "I sure hope that doesn't happen at the parade!"

9

The Main Event

I dashed back to the barn. Suddenly I felt nervous.

"Comet, can I ask you something?" I said as I stood in front of her stall.

"Sure, Bo," she said. "You know you can ask me anything."

"Why did you chase that squirrel?" I asked.

"Because you taught me to," Comet answered. "I did a good job, didn't I? I scared it away."

Oh no. I pawed at the straw on the floor. Now I felt terrible.

"Um, Comet," I whimpered, "I don't think I'm such a good horse teacher.

I know a lot about the farm. I know all about being a dog. But I don't know much about being a horse. You should forget everything I taught you."

I turned to leave, but Star and Grey were standing behind me. I hadn't heard them come in.

"Bo, you may not know about being
a horse, but you know a lot about
being a good friend," Star said. "And
that's exactly what Comet needs."

Grey nodded, then faced Comet.
"And you, young foal—we saw you
walking with the kids outside. Your

mother and I have never been more proud of you. You did a terrific job, and we know you are going to do great at the parade today."

The family nuzzled noses.

Now I felt warm and fuzzy inside,
just as Darnell and Jennica, my human
dad and mom, joined us in the barn.

It was time for the parade. They led
Comet out to the trailer.

As I watched her walk away, I wished more than anything that I could go with Comet. Then Jennica came back to the barn, and she was holding . . . my leash! I was going to go with Comet!

It was very crowded at the fairground.
People were everywhere, but I could
still walk easily through the park with
my family.

There were so many new smells swirling all around me. I sniffed salty, buttery popcorn; yummy, meaty hamburgers; and sweet, grassy hay! The scents were all mixed together, dancing in the air.

Imani and Wyatt went on a few rides. And there was an art show with pictures hung up in a small gallery outdoors.

One painting looked just like a giant bone. Maybe it *was* a giant bone!

I was about to take a test bite when a loud voice announced, "Ladies and gentlemen, girls and boys, it's time for the Foal Show!"

Jennica and Darnell led me over to the show area. It looked like the school back at our farm.

We watched as, one by one, a line of kids walked their foals around the ring. Parents stood outside the fence clapping happily. All the foals looked so proud as they trotted by, though a few were a bit startled when they spotted me.

Finally, Imani and Comet came out. Comet's mane was smooth and silky, her coat glistened in the sunlight, and all the dust had been brushed from her legs.

As she walked around the ring, I kept a close lookout for squirrels, but luckily none appeared. I gave a happy woof as Comet walked by me.

Comet grinned a horsey grin and winked as she went past. My puppy heart beat so fast. I couldn't wait to tell all the animals back on the farm about it.

Raised in a Barn

Back home, I helped Imani and Wyatt get Comet down from the trailer and take her back to the stall.

They both patted her on the neck and fished out some carrots for her.

"You did such a good job today, Comet," Imani said. "You get the rest of the week off!"

When the kids left, I stayed behind.
My tail wagged fast because I was
bursting with pride and excitement.

"Guess what, Comet!" I shouted. "Some of the other horses got so surprised when they saw me that they forgot where they were! Just like what happened when you saw that squirrel earlier. But not you. You did great!"

Comet laughed and said, "I guess horses just don't like surprises so much."

Now it was my turn to laugh. "Hmm, then I don't think you're going to like this!"

I darted out of the stall, and Comet trotted after me.

"SURPRISE!" everyone shouted.

All the animals on the farm gathered together to celebrate Comet's big day.

Comet told everyone about the foal parade, and I told everyone about the fair.

Then Star and Grey told us about the first show they walked in when they were foals. That was where they met and fell in love!

Then, farm animals being farm animals, everyone had a story to share. And as I listened to my friends, that warm and fuzzy feeling began to fill me up again.

I was one lucky pup to be raised in a barn like this.

Here's a peek at Bo's next big adventure!

GOOD D🐾G

Herd You Loud and Clear

How in the world do sheep stay so fluffy—no matter what they do?

Whenever I spend the day playing outside in the field, my fur gets tangled and wild. If I take a nap lying against a tree, my fur is smooshed flat and totally dirty when I wake up.

An excerpt from *Herd You Loud and Clear*

And I don't even want to tell you what happens when I roll around in the barn.

But sheep are different from dogs. No matter what they do, they are always puffy. Their wool seems to stay bouncy and cheerful like a cloud all the time.

There is just one problem. Even though they look super soft, sheep do *not* like to be used as pillows. I learned that the hard way.

There is something that sheep *do* love: playing hide-and-seek. And that was what we were doing on a sunny afternoon.

An excerpt from *Herd You Loud and Clear*

My buddy Puffs was hiding. I was seeking.

Puffs is a very nice sheep, and he's a really good friend. But he's not the best at playing hide-and-seek.

When he's the seeker, he almost always forgets that we are playing a game. If something catches his eye, he'll wander over to check it out and forget to come find me!

And if he is the one hiding, well, let's just say he doesn't always remember how fluffy and white he is . . . and it's hard enough to find good hiding spots in an open green field.

An excerpt from *Herd You Loud and Clear*